THE CRISIS IN 9-E

NAMAN A

Made with ♥ on the Notion Press Platform
www.notionpress.com

Contents

Contents

FOREWORD

Life within the walls of a school often feels predictable—a blend of bustling classrooms, whispered secrets, and the relentless rhythm of bells. But sometimes, even the most familiar places can become the setting for the unexpected. This book explores the extraordinary experiences of a group of students who find themselves at the center of a whirlwind of mysteries, dangers, and revelations.

As you dive into the chapters ahead, you will uncover a tale that transcends the usual boundaries of school life. It is a story of resilience and courage, where ordinary students are thrown into extraordinary circumstances. From nail-biting investigations to heart-stopping counter-insurgency operations, the journey of Class 9-E with the APDI (Academy of Prime Detectives of India) will leave you gripping the pages.

This is not just a story about what happens when youthful curiosity collides with hidden truths. It is about friendship, determination, and the courage to face adversities that seem insurmountable. With every twist and turn, you will find yourself drawn deeper into a world where the lines between right and wrong, friend and foe, blur into shades of gray.

Welcome to the world of **THE CRISIS IN 9-E**. May the adventure begin!

PREFACE

In the hallowed halls of Golden Valley Public School, the innocence of school life meets the chilling reality of unforeseen dangers. What starts as a series of bizarre accidents escalates into a high-stakes mystery, entwining the lives of Class 9-E with forces far beyond their comprehension. With each incident, the students are drawn closer to a hidden conspiracy. The APDI bridges their classroom and the perilous world of counter-insurgency operations. Combining humor, suspense, and heart-pounding action, this book explores what happens when school students and an APDI agent face extraordinary challenges. This is a story of courage, unity, and uncovering the truth, no matter the cost.

ACKNOWLEDGEMENTS

I thank my parents and teachers for encouraging me to write my 3rd book. I also thank CHATGPT and GOOGLE for the real accounts and images for my book. I also thank my best-friend Rishabh to give me good ideas on crucial points. I also thank my grandfather (maternal) to preview my book. THANK YOU to all the people who helped me in making of this book.

Prologue

It was supposed to be another typical school year at Golden Valley Public School, but fate had other plans for Class 9-E. A collapsing steel shed, suspicious fires, and eerie coincidences began to paint a sinister picture. At first, it seemed like an unfortunate string of events—until a coded message hidden in plain sight unraveled a far deeper threat. As an APDI agent, Karan and his other agents stumble upon secrets meant to stay buried, they find themselves thrust into a web of lies and danger extending far beyond their school grounds. Their investigation collides with a covert counter-insurgency operation, where a shadowy adversary lurks, waiting to strike. What follows is a battle of wits and survival, as the students and their unlikely allies fight to protect not just their school but their very lives.

ASSEMBLY GONE WRONG!

A SPINE-CHILLING ACCIDENT THAT ALMOST DESTROYED RISHAN

I

9-E REUNITES

IN THE PERSPECTIVE OF RISHAN:

Today marked the end of my two-week winter break, and I found myself waking up at 7 AM, an hour I had nearly forgotten existed during my lazy days of sleeping in until 11. Adjusting to an early morning after such a long pause was a challenge, and I felt the heaviness of sleep still clinging to me like a warm blanket.

As I stumbled out of bed, I could sense the remnants of my holiday routine lingering. The thought of returning to school filled me with a mix of anticipation and dread. After nearly two weeks of lounging around, it was hard to shake off the cosy lethargy that had settled into my bones.

Still in a daze, I shuffled to the bathroom, half awake and desperate for a proper wake-up call. In a moment of sleepiness, I found myself brushing my teeth with shampoo instead of toothpaste. The minty freshness of my usual routine was replaced by the unexpected, and slightly unsettling, taste of my shampoo. It wasn't until I caught a glimpse of myself in the mirror, toothbrush in hand, that I realized my comedic blunder. Making it more funnier. Later, I shampooed my hair with toothpaste, making my hair stiff.

I chuckled at my sleep-deprived antics, a gentle reminder of how I needed to transition back to the school routine. With a little more alertness, I finally managed to brush my teeth correctly, wash my hair, and prepare for the day ahead, albeit with a bit of a giggle still stuck in my throat about my earlier mix-up.

I just wanted to escape from sleep, so I stood under the shower and rotated the knob. My body went chill when cold water drenched my body. I just jumped out of surprise when I felt the cold water instead of being treated with muscle-relieving warm water. I was in a cold shower for 3 seconds in a 17-degree(celsius) atmosphere on Jan 3! HORRIBLE!

I realised that I rotated the wrong knob. I closed the knob and stepped out of the shower area. Then, I rotated the correct knob, checked the temperature of the water, and stepped in. The relief I got when I was exposed to warm water was indescribable and pleasurable. But, I was still in a sleepy mood.

After shampooing my hair with Colgate(as already mentioned above), I stepped out, wore my uniform, and went to have my breakfast. You'd be thinking about how I shampooed my hair with Colgate, right? Let me explain briefly.

Actually, my mother bought a product online that looked the same as a shampoo container. My mother bought it to store Colgate in it to make our daily routines simple and hassle-free. Both, the shampoo container and the Colgate container were kept nearby, perplexing me. Which eventually led me to brush my teeth with shampoo and shampoo my hair with Colgate.

Now just forget about shampoo and toothpaste. My mother prepared Idly-Sambhar for breakfast. I was still not prepared for the day because I dipped Idly in water instead of dipping it in Sambhar! Disgusting! I just prayed to god that none of my enemies get this kind of morning as I got today. I just hoped my day would go well.

After many more mishaps, I was ready to board my school bus. The Golden Valley Public School's bus arrived with a horn. I stepped on the bus and sat on the second-last seat. Someone slapped me from behind. The slap was rough and fast, but not hard. I turned back and saw my best friend, Virag. He came in front(near me) and talked a lot with me.

GVPS

After an hour, we reached the 'GOLDEN VALLEY PUBLIC SCHOOL'(GVPS). GVPS is one of India's best schools and the largest school in Coimbatore! It possesses five academic blocks and an indoor stadium. My school was unimaginably huge. It contains a Football field, hockey courts(2), Basketball courts(2), Volleyball courts(2), a swimming pool, a Cricket ground, and five badminton courts. Amazing, right?!

We also have a large auditorium and each block has its assembly hall. The reason for my school being that huge is that it lies in the Outskirts of Coimbatore.

Coimbatore

The school environment for some is very easy to adapt to, but for 'others', it is truly tough. I come under the category of 'others'. Virag and I greeted our class teacher, Ms. Salia Dinshaw(also our chem teacher), and had our seats. We were the last to enter the class.

Aryan seemed to be fine, though he had met with an operation of 'Umbullical-Hernia' the previous month. Vivaan was oddly silent. But the Agarwal brothers, Neeraj Agarwal and Suraj Agarwal were as usually making noise. All others looked equally happy.

After the prayer, Ms Dinshaw announced that Alia, Kiara and Nayra had planned for our assembly and were ready to share the points. All the boys were uninterested in it but there was no choice. We had to perform the assembly. The topic was interesting, but we didn't like it.

The assembly was going to be about submerged continents like Kumari-Kandam and Zealandia. According to their plan, we were to breach the content through a skit. The skit was to be composed of a Geography teacher and 10 students. The girls agreed to their plan without any hitch. But we boys were MADE to agree to their plan.

After some further discussions, we moved towards character allocation, which was completed smoothly. Next was the creation of a classroom environment on the stage. Many had divergent opinions on it. But after a heated debate, it was concluded that:

1. A wall of cardboard is to be made,
2. There will be 8 desks and chairs,
3. One teacher table in front of the blackboard and,
4. The blackboard is to be made of cardboard.

Everything was set. Now only practice and cooperation were required. We made a note of our dialogues and their timings. As soon as we completed writing our dialogues, the bell rang and the Hindi period started. Ms Salia bid us goodbye and left the class and our Hindi teacher arrived

II

A JUMP GONE WRONG

THE NEXT DAY(JAN 4):

My morning was better than yesterday. Fortunately, I faced zero mishaps. Today, Dosa chutney was served for breakfast. Though being a Rajasthani, I don't know why, but my mother is obsessed with South Indian dishes.

I entered the class and observed everyone. All neutral (emotions). Our first period was maths and Ms Shakuntala was already waiting for Ms Dinshaw to leave the class. The 45-minute long period got over and our games period started. I always wished, and continue to wish that our PT teacher, Mr Ken were as punctual as Ms Shakuntala is. He always arrived 5-10 minutes late to our class.

Today, Mr Ken auditioned for an inter-school competition for Long jump. Chirag outperformed me by only 2 cm. Ah!!!!! I was frustrated and upset because I lost by only 2 cm. We left the ground and were back to class. Annoyed by my jump, I tried to jump again in the class with Virag. I thrusted up high and landed on the wet floor!

I slipped and my forehead hit one of the benches and fell. The collision was impactful; After the collision, my body tilted to the right and fell on my back. Virag quickly reached his hand to help me. I clasped his hand with mine and stood up. Blood gushed out. I applied pressure on the wound with my hand to slow down the blood loss.

Virag grabbed my hand and we descended to the infirmary room. With my half-closed blurry eyes, I spotted that the nurse was dealing with another boy, who was probably suffering from stomach ache. She left him and rushed towards me. She cleaned the wound and examined it. She applied a bandage and urged me to leave for home but I refused and she informed my parents about it.

I took some rest there in the infirmary for an hour and returned to my class. Ms Salia was taking class. She asked about the pain and ordered me to take some rest. She didn't ask about how, when and where I got the wound. Probably, Chirag would've informed about it to mam.

DURING LUNCH:

"Hey bro!" I called Virag.
"What?" Virag asked.
"I am a bit perplexed about my fall,"
"Why?"
"Cuz, I was the one leaving the class last and entering the class first but the whole floor was dry."
"Hmmmm...... Maybe you would've missed it,"
"No bro, I certainly did check perfectly!"

"Maybe some teacher would've spilt the water accidentally,"

"Okay, then they would've surely called the janitor to clean it up."

"Maybe, but....." Before he completed, Salia mam announced that she had borrowed this period for assembly rehearsal.

AT HOME:

"Mom! I am back,"

"Oh my son, what had happened to you? I was so restless and tensed about it,"

"Nothing serious, I just fell while playing Football. That's all." (I didn't reveal the actual reason)

"What? You fell while playing, how? Where? When? and why?"

"Mom, mom, just relax. Only a small wound."

Tears filled in my mother's eyes and she hugged me tightly. The whole day my mother pampered me a lot.

III
WHEN THE DEATH FAILS

ON JAN 11:

It was a rainy morning. The rain was lashing the city of Coimbatore from the previous night itself. My wound was almost recovered and there were no traces of pain. Though the morning was rainy, I was still a sleepy head. Today, I proved my mother correct and proved myself as a dumb-head. My mother used to call me a dumb-head and I proved it correct today.

I will show you the list of dumb things I did this morning:

1. I shampooed my hair with body wash and washed my body with shampoo.
2. Brushed my teeth with my father's toothbrush.
3. Combed my hair with my pet dog Tommy's hairbrush.

Frustrating, isn't it? No? Then there's more. I wore two different socks and got late to my school. So, I insisted my father drop me off to school, making my father annoyed. All this happened because I had no sleep the previous night as there was heavy construction going on in the neighbourhood.

By the way, tomorrow was the day of assembly and today we would rehearse it on the stage. So, I hoped the day would go good. But I was unaware that it was going to be the worst day in my whole life.

Astonishingly, I reached the school before my school bus did. I walked past the main gate, entered my block and then my class. Ms Salia was not there in the class. I took my seat and started discussing about assembly with Neel. After a few minutes, Virag came in and then Ms Salia. The rain was nearing to stop.

After prayer, Ms Salia announced that we would be setting the set-up for the assembly right now on the stage and rehearsing. Though we should have been practicing only after lunch, but we were doing it before lunch itself because Ms Salia had some work in the afternoon. Cardboard and benches were already sent down, our only work was to set them on the stage.

We set the benches and desks on the stage and got down. Salia mam sent me to the stage to check for the view and angle. I sat on the bench set up in the middle of the stage. Suddenly Salia mam shouted my name with her face up. Following her gaze, I saw that the steel shed was crashing down just above me!

I quickly reacted and tried to hide under the desk swiftly. While ducking, the right side of my forehead and right arm got injured. The steel roof crashed on the desks and benches.

NARRATOR:

The steel shed was placed 3 floors above the ground. It weighed around 4-5 tonnes, and that hit the stage where Rishan was present. The impact of the collision was so devastating that all the benches and desks broke, some from the middle while some crumbled. But to Rishan's luck, the bench above him did not break but bent and hit him.

The impact also affected the wooden stage. The wooden stage was covered with carpet. The stage also broke in many areas. The sight when the steel shed crashed was frightening enough to give you pyloerection (goosebumps). A very loud noise was produced. It was difficult to say whether Rishan broke some of his bones or his life itself.

There was complete silence after the accident. Don't know, whether of shock or surprise. It suddenly started to rain. Virag broke into tears and ran towards the stage (broken). Following him, others too came. They tried their level best to lift the steel shed but were unsuccessful. Ms Salia was frozen in shock and the trauma was terrible!

RISHAN:

While ducking, the right side of my forehead and my right arm got injured. Blood was gushing out from my forehead. While ducked, the desk above me bent and hit my spine, giving me intense pain. The impact made on my spine made me rest on the steel support of the desk with my stomach. The stage too, broke just near me and one of the protruding wood planks almost went through me, enough to kill me.

I was suffering from intense pain. Since my stomach was resting on a steel rod, it gave me unbearable pain. I was unable to move because all of my energy and stamina was eradicated. But somehow, I moved front to escape injuring my stomach. While I moved, my whole body pained and made a loud grunt. Now I had no energy to open my eyes also.

I was breathing heavily, but not as heavily as it was downpouring now. It was raining unbelievably heavily, drenching me out completely with cold water at 20°C. Fierce torture! My friends were constantly calling out my name but I didn't have the energy to speak. One-fourth of my face was covered with blood. I was slowly fainting and I fainted.

VIRAG:

We all were trying to push the shed but there was no use. I thought for a few minutes. An idea clicked! I called Vivaan and Neeraj and explained them about my plan. Vivaan and I went to the side. We tried to go beneath the benches and desks. It was tough to move forward because the benches and desks were broken and the stage was very irregular. Every move we made was very careful. Even one mistake, the desks would fall on us or the planks of the stage would kill us.

After hard work of 10 minutes, we spotted Rishan. We were in seventh heaven. We tried to wake him up but he didn't. Cold sweat passed through us. We again and again tried to wake him but he didn't. I moved more forward and grabbed his waist, while Vivaan caught his arms. Slowly-slowly we pulled him back. After hard work of 15 minutes, Rishan's face was visible to the whole world.

Luckily he was breathing. Neeraj further helped us to pull Rishan out. We were successful! But all were still trying to move the steel shed. But one loud call from Vivaan grabbed everyone's attention. Nurse Sarah rushed and first cleaned the wound on his forehead and his right arm.

Finally, ward boys with a stretcher emerged. They loaded him on the stretcher and transferred him to the ambulance. The principal went with Rishan.

PRINCIPAL:

Rishan was taken to the CSG Hospital, which is one of the best and one of the largest hospitals in India. The hospital wasn't far, it was only 3 kilometers but those 3 kilometers were like 30 kilometers! The doctor inside the ambulance gave an injection and slowly Rishan gained consciousness. He was made to wear oxygen while we reached the hospital.

CSG Hospital

They transferred Rishan to the hospital and administered a butterfly needle for IV (Intra-Venous-Glucose drips). They took him for a complete check-up. From bones to muscles, from ligaments to skin. He was checked completely and it was a miracle that he didn't suffer from any fractures! It was unbelievable! He only sustained a muscle strain, a ligament strain, a stretch on the stomach, stitches on the forehead and some blood-clotting in the legs.

When Rishan came out from the scan room, his parents arrived. The doctor explained everything to his parents and informed them that he would be discharged tomorrow. It was a very good news! They shifted Rishan to the General Ward. Rishan's father became angry and questioned me about the safety of the students. I explained him everything and he was calm. His father was tensed and afraid but he handled the situation smoothly.

I guaranteed the students' safety and also promised that I would bear all the costs and provide compensation for the mental damage and trauma. Surprisingly, they refused the compensation, and though I forced them a lot, they didn't agree.

Rishan:

Later that day, many of my friends and Ms Salia paid a visit and broke out the news that the school would remain closed for 10 days and would conduct an inspection. My parents were happy with this move, and so was I.

THE NEXT DAY (JAN 12):

The doctor visited me and explained that I would be able to recover fully after 8-12 days. He also gave us prescriptions for the medicines and explained other stuff about diet and exercise. Later that day, I was discharged from the hospital and I returned to my home. It was so peaceful in my house. My mother again started to pamper me and served me all my favourite cuisine but within the limits of the diet given by the doctor.

Again my friends visited me with a get-well-soon card and a bouquet. The Principal too visited my house and asked for my wellness. It was hard to digest that I survived such a terrific accident without any major damage. It was truly unbelievable and indescribable!

CHEMISTRY ON FIRE

ANOTHER FIERY ACCIDENT

IV
RUMOUR CLAIMED TRUE

KARNIK:

JAN 23:

Finally, after 10 long days, the school was reopening after the inspection period. Something was suspicious about the shed fall. While I was trying to move the shed, I noticed curved edges that didn't align with the rest of the border. So, maybe it was deliberately done for some reason.

But why only our class? (9-E) The water spill, and the shed fall during our assembly rehearsals. The shed fall was indeed horrifying. It almost killed Rishan. I wasn't feeling comfortable in the school. There was something suspicious.

When I entered the class, there was pitch silence. It was very unusual for our class to not make any noise. Probably, all were still horrified by the incidents. Though the steel shed was replaced and fixed, but the stage wasn't repaired yet.

It was very awkward to sit in a very silent class which used to be a very vociferous class. It could also be because Rishan and Vivaan were absent. Virag told me that Rishan was stable now and would come by the 24th or 25th. It was a miracle that he withstood the accident.

JAN 25:

As I entered the class today, it seemed that everyone had forgotten about the accident and had come back to normal. When I analysed the class, I knew why all were normal. Because Rishan and Vivaan were present today! Rishan looked as healthy as he was on Jan 3. The level of my happiness was high when I spotted them together.

We all talked a lot and returned to our home.

JAN 31:

Today, Neel was absent, so I was made to sit near Nithin on the bus. He is an 11th-grader. He told me a story which was very interesting but was more like a rumour but was claimed as true by him. It was related to our school, indeed our block. There's a class on the 2nd floor, 8-C. There's a weird thing. 8th standard is on the 2nd floor while 9th standard was on the 1st floor. Both are in the same block.

"You know, during the construction of our block, they made a very big mistake and realised it only after the construction was completed. Left to class 8-C, is the store room. When they realised, it was too late." Nithin said.

"Oh! What mistake did our school make? I am feeling very curious!" I expressed.

"So, the store room and 8-C share a wall. But during construction, they made a non-grilled window, which was not supposed to be built there. To hide it, they temporarily fixed a wooden plank. It was only a temporary setting, but they forgot about it and to hide it, they kept a movable cupboard." He conveyed.

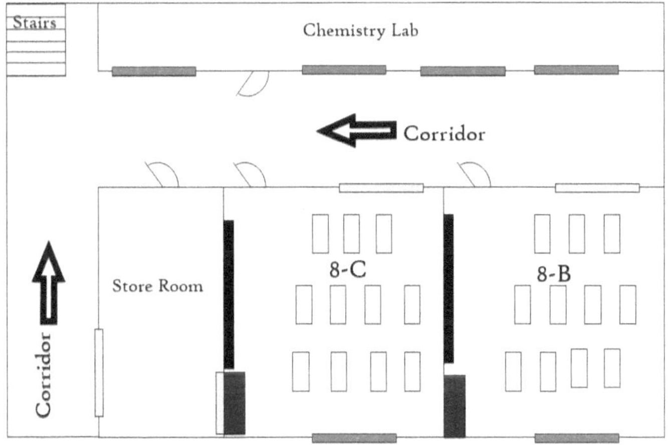

LAYOUT (dark gray-grilled windows; light gray-non-griled windows)

It sounded more like a myth than a true incident. I felt so, because who could make such a blunder? It's impossible. Though, it managed to catch my mind for the whole day!

On the bus, while returning to home, I sat near Nithin again. He recited some more intriguing stories. Although his stories were interesting, they were rumours which Nithin claimed it were true. That night, his stories didn't allow me to sleep, forcing me to think about it.

The next day Neel came and I missed the other stories which Nithin had promised me that he will convey it to me.

V

THE FAULTY SMART BOARD

FEB 1:

Today in the class, there was a 22nd person. 20 students (incl. me), Ms Salia and the technician Vaibhav. He was checking the smart board. Oh yeah! I forgot to say that all the classes in the school had smart boards for effective learning. Vaibhav sir fixed the problem in 10 minutes and explained the problem for another 10 minutes.

Later that day, we had a problem with the smart board. Not once; Not twice; Not thrice but four times! Here is the list of all the times the problem occurred:

1. Before everyone arrived at the school.
2. After the library period.
3. After the computer lab period.
4. After the art period, and

5. After the games period.

Suspiciously, all five times we had the same problem. Literally the fifth time, Neel fixed the problem! When I further investigated, I noticed that whenever the problem arose, no one was present in the class. Which made me conclude that it was done purposefully to aggravate us. But why only 9-E?

A Smart board

In the end, the question remained unsolved and I then boarded the bus. The whole time I was thinking about it. Though after reaching home I forgot about it, but as soon as I comforted myself on the bed, the question flashed in my mind repeatedly. Due to this, I hardly slept.

FEB 3:

Now tell me, what is the worse? I'll give you two choices:

1. Standing outside for punishment at 12 noon, or
2. Not sleeping for the past two days.

Some may prefer the first choice, while most of them would opt for the second one. But in my fate, I got the experience of both things TOGETHER! Confused? I will explain:

For the past 2 days, I hardly slept due to the unsolved question of the smart board malfunction. I was standing outside for the past 50 minutes as punishment. I got it because I argued with Ms Laswell, (General Knowledge teacher) who was from the UK and was a pro-Western*. (*In context to this book, it meant countries lying in the western hemisphere. Like Europe and America)

I will explain why I argued with Ms Laswell. Ms Laswell was pro-Western and could not tolerate talks against the West. Mam was taking a class about Newton's Laws of Motion. She was boasting too much about Newton. I became intolerant and just said the following:-

"The recent news reports said that Maharishi Kanad in the 5th or 6th century BCE, mentioned the Laws of Motion in Sanskrit before Newton, mam"

Just for saying this, she got offended and sent me out of the class. Ms Laswell had the 4th and 5th period and she sent me out by 11:10 and it was around 12:10 when she called me in. Oh yeah! Ms Laswell took us to 8-C because of the Board issue. The whole floor (10 classes) was empty because all the 8th-grade students were on the ground for a seminar. So it was only 20 students and 1 teacher on the whole floor.

Left to 8-C is the store room and 8-B is to its right. The chemistry lab was opposite to 8-C. It was 12:20, 20 minutes to lunch. I was half-asleep when I suddenly got startled when I heard a loud metallic noise. It was not the sound of the bell.

I was sitting near the window to the corridor. I peeped out to see that two peons were on the floor, struggling. I analysed and inferred that one peon was carrying a bucket full of oil to the store room. (Maybe for some puja) When another peon popped out from the store room and hit the peon with oil, making the whole floor covered with oil.

The oil was spilt on the closed doors of the storeroom and 8-C. Even the major part of the corridor in front of the class was covered with oil and was about to reach the Chemistry lab. Also, the water filler machine and the water cans (20 L) near the class were not affected by the oil.

Surprisingly, neither of the peons was familiar to any of us. Ms Laswell went out to give them a piece of her mind in English. I was certain that they wouldn't understand a single word she said, but I hoped they would at least grasp the idea that they needed to clean the floor.

Both the unknown peons went down to the first floor to grab the cloth to clean the floor, though there were cleaning clothes on every floor. Suspicious. 5-minutes passed, but there were no clues about those peons. We cannot leave the class also because the oil was spilt in the major part of the corridor.

It was 12:30, 10 minutes for lunch. There were no traces of those peons. Ms Laswell was chatting with girls and I was bored of being quiet for long. So, I turned towards Akhil to discuss about the new car that Lamborghini unveiled yesterday. I just murmured and Ms Laswell made me stand! Ahhhhhhhhhhhh!!!!!!!!!!!!

As I stood, a deafening sound and a very bright light, made us blind and deaf for a moment or two. All the windows in the classroom shattered. There was perfect chaos in the classroom. All the girls and Ms Laswell shrieked and cried. Glass shards were all over my desk. Even the smart board had cracks and got powered off.

I turned towards the Chemistry lab to see the flames! There was an explosion in the chemistry lab. Fortunately, the flames didn't reach the classroom (for now). It was almost 120 seconds until we could process anything. We decided to leave the class. Then I remembered the oil spill incident and peeped out of the window to see that the fire was very close to our class! I shared this with everyone and asked everyone to remain in the class.

While I peeped out, the smoke went inside my lungs and my whole face was covered with soot particles and sweat. My eyes were burning and teary.

We moved away from the window. Smoke started to enter the class and the class door caught fire! Seeing this, everyone started to shout and got frightened. Now there was no way that we could escape this. Many of them started to cry, while some were tough. There was an outside chance that we could live.

Just to increase our survival, we boys shifted the benches and desks away from the wall. We all sat on the floor to avoid inhalation of smoke. We were busy thinking about how to escape the blaze, but some were busy crying loudly.

Suddenly, an idea struck Aryan's mind and he shared it with us. As we have water cans near the water filler machines, we could use them to tackle the fire. There should be around 5 to 6 20-litre water cans. Nice idea. But the problem was, who would go to the LoDS? (Line of Death and Survival)

We didn't inform our plan to Ms Laswell because she won't allow for this. So we kept this a secret. After 2-3 minutes, Anurag announced to us (boys) that he was ready to take this risk. This was a very courageous decision. For now, LoDS was the most dangerous place on Earth and Anurag was the most courageous boy. (only for a while)

The plan was:-

We would stick the desk to the wall in front of the window to the corridor. Anurag would step on it and go out to collect those cans. He would pass it to us (Vivaan, Virag and me). This may seem simple, but it was not. Anurag was going to the line between death and survival. (Line: The corridor; Life: 8-C; Death: Fiery part of Chem lab and the corridor)

The Chem lab

We told this plan to Nayra so that she could keep Ms Laswell busy and doesn't notice us. Rishan quietly kept the desk near the window because the glass shards were spread all over the floor and the platform of the window. We (Anurag, Vivaan, Virag and me) drenched our kerchieves and placed it around our faces so that soot particles don't enter our lungs.

VI
BREATHING FUMES

ANURAG:

The bench was ready; I was ready; and the LoDS was ready to engulf me. I drenched my kerchief and covered my face. Neel poured 2-3 bottles of water on me so that I could prevent myself from getting burns. I climbed the bench and walked steadily. Smoke irritated my eyes brutally. I made a small jump and landed in the corridor. I was only able to see fire and smoke. I doubted if the water cans survived.

It was hard to breathe. Burning eyes and irritated nose made it difficult to do the mission. To worsen the things, itching troubled my body. I started walking toward the water filler machine. I spotted it and to my surprise, it was safe! WOAH! I grabbed one and dragged it towards the window. It was very heavy and truly hot. OUCH!

When the window came, I lifted it and handed it to Vivaan and Karnik who were inside the class, ready to grab it. I did the same for the other four cans too. While leaving, I spotted a 8-litre bucket. I took that and handed it to Virag. The extreme heat was killing me. I was breathing fumes! Now the time was to get back to class through the window.

I was fainting. I was barely able to stand. Vivaan quickly passed me a chair and I stepped on it, then on the desk, and finally, I was on the ground of 8-C. As soon as I entered the class, I was surrounded by applause. And, as soon as I stepped on the ground of 8-C, I fell and almost fainted when Rishan poured 2 bottles of water on me. The boys made me sit straight and gave me water to drink. RELIEF!

I escaped the LoDS and the CoET (Corridor of Extreme Torture). I escaped the heat torture. My clothes and my face went pitch black due to the soot particles of fire. A bucket full of water was poured on me. The water was warm, but it gave me relief and some soot particles drained. It was hard to believe that I survived the LoDS. There was only coughing, and irritation in my nose, eyes and hair. No burns!

Our hopes revived and everyone stopped crying. This itself was a very big achievement. The smoke filled the room, but it also escaped through the window facing the assembly hall. My brain was exploding with thinking, thinking and thinking!

KARNIK:

It was 1:10 PM. No one was there to help us. Maybe everyone of the other class students were unaware of our presence in the second floor. They would've assumed that we were somewhere else. There was one strange thing. Why didn't the sprinklers work? This was a tough question.

We all drank water from time to time to maintain our body temperature. One thing was clear we shouldn't wait for the fire-fighters to arrive and help us. Suddenly, the fire started to spread on the walls. Everyone started to panic and there was chaos in the room. By seeing this chaos, My brain recalled Nithin's story. If you remember, he told me a story about the ungrilled window to the storeroom. We could break the plank and from the window to the corridor (another one) from the storeroom, we could escape!

I shared this with Ms Laswell. She agreed to my proposal unwillingly because there were no options left. If the rumour came true, (which became my hope) we all would be saved. If my hope didn't work......

While I was sharing with Ms Laswell; Alia overheard our conversation, and took a paper and made two sets of paper chits with numbers written in it. When mam agreed to my plan, she made girls take the chit, then to the boys. I realised that those chits decided the order in which we would exit the class.

She had made 2 sets of chits from 1 to 10 and gave one set to girls and the other one to boys. My fate decided that I would be the last one to exit the class because '10' was written on my chit. Ahhhhh!!!!!!!!

Neel, Rishan, Vivaan, Suraj and I were trying to move the cupboard. But the cupboard liked its own place and it didn't move. So we decided to let the cupboard fall. So we five applied pressure from one single side on the top and the cupboard fell. We all jumped in joy when the cupboard was in pieces. Anurag and Virag cleared the pieces of wood.

To my surprise, Nithin's story was 90% True. No wooden planks were covering the window but he mentioned the wooden plank. The window didn't shatter but had cracks.

When I tried to open it, it didn't. Vivaan kicked the frame of the window and it opened. As it opened, smoke escaped from the storeroom. I coughed and quickly bent down to avoid the smoke. Now the smoke was entering from the corridor and the storeroom. I waited for the smoke to escape. Then I entered the storeroom as soon as the smoke reduced.

It was horrific to see that fire was only 6-7 metres away from the window! I quickly opened the other window to the corridor. (It was a private window) It opened without any problems. From the classroom, Vivaan passed me 3 chairs. I placed it in front of both the windows and placed the other one outside in the corridor for convenience in climbing and stepping down.

The burning store room

While I was entering the class, I spotted 6 woollen blankets, which could be used to resist the fire. I quickly grabbed it and entered the class.

VII
WATER IS LIFE

RISHAN:

Karnik burst into the class, his arms were laden with five or six thick woollen blankets, each one seemingly too heavy for a single person to carry. His face was streaked with soot, his breath ragged, yet his voice carried an unyielding authority as he quickly explained the dire situation. The faint crackling of flames from the storeroom seeped into our ears, a chilling reminder of what was at stake.

"We don't have time to panic," Karnik said, his words slicing through the haze of fear. "Virag, you and him,"—his finger jabbed toward me—"grab the water cans and buckets. You're tackling this head-on."

The air was heavy, thick with anticipation and smoke that seemed to claw its way into the room.

Virag and I entered the storeroom with a water can and a bucket. We had drenched our kerchieves and masked them around our faces for protection.

Virag tore the seal off the can with a decisive twist and began pouring water into the bucket. As soon as it was filled, I hurled the contents toward the flames. The fire hissed and recoiled, but it was far from defeated. Sweat dripped down my forehead, mixing with the ash that clung to our skin. The room was a battleground, and the fire was relentless.

Each splash of water felt like a drop in the ocean, yet we pressed on. The air grew thicker, our lungs burning with each desperate breath. My scalp itched from the heat, and my vision blurred, but there was no stopping now.

One by one, others managed to escape. The class was emptying, but we were far from safe. "Another can!" I yelled hoarsely, my voice barely cutting through the roar of the fire. Akhil, from the class, slid one toward us with a precision born of desperation.

Minutes felt like hours. By now, Virag had taken over the splashing while I filled the buckets. The fire, though still fierce, began to wane under our relentless assault.

Only five of us remained: Virag, Akhil, Vivaan, Ms. Laswell, and me. My voice cracked as I suggested, "We leave once the others are out."

Reluctantly, Virag nodded. We passed the half-empty can and bucket to Aryan, who stood anxiously in the corridor. Vivaan handed me three more cans, their weight nearly buckling my knees, and I passed them to Aryan and Anurag, who quickly retreated to safety.

Akhil appeared with two woollen blankets in his arms. "Wrap up," he urged, thrusting them into our hands. The coarse fabric scratched against my skin as we draped them over ourselves, bracing for whatever came next.

Ms Laswell, with the support of Akhil's shoulder, climbed the chair, went past the window and stepped on the other chair. She got down and climbed the other chair with the support of my shoulder. Went past the window, reached the corridor and went to the farthest end from the fire. Vivaan and Akhil too left. Virag, with my confirmation, left. I checked the classroom once. All out. I too left the classroom and entered the corridor. I hugged Virag (he was waiting for me) in joy and we celebrated our survival and went to the farthest end. I turned back to see the horrific sight of fire, it was scary!

The burning corridor

All of them were happy and were celebrating their second life! There were tears of joy and relief. The happiness of getting a second life was too much to take in. Though it was the third one for me. It was better here because there was no smoke and was a bit chill compared to 8-C. It was calm and peaceful there. My lungs finally got good and purified air after hours of hardwork.

But the problem didn't end. We were to reach the ground. But both the stairs were inaccessible. One was flaming, while the other one (near us) was demolished for renovation purposes. The staircase was of wood, so the school decided to swap it with a concrete one for safety purposes. Meaning, we were stuck again!

The joy didn't last long when we discovered that we were stuck again. The proverb, "Nothing is Permanent in Life!" was executed on us. Because all our happiness and joy washed away when I shared this with everyone. Their joyful faces were converted into frowned ones. Everyone panicked. My Brain stopped Braining. Thoughts flashed in my mind at the speed of light, Not of surviving, but of dying.

I willed to die instead of just straining my Brain, muscles, lungs and every single nerve just for the happiness of a few seconds. There were only problems. Before we could solve one, another arose. If solved, the happiness doesn't last long. There was a will to die.

A tear dropped from my eye. My eyes watered. Everything went blurry because of the tears. The tears eventually ended up as sobs. The struggle we did to escape the fire was slowly going in vain as smoke emerged. All started crying again. Even if we shout to our fellow students down on the other side of the ground, they won't hear it. It was so because the constant noise produced by the fire fainted our voices.

NARRATOR:

While all of them lost their courage and were remembering their loved ones, Karnik stood confident and hopeful. In a moment wrapped in despair, he was the sole figure of determination, a beacon amidst the shadows of fear that enveloped his companions. The atmosphere was thick with anxiety—the air thick with unspoken fears and the weight of memories. Eyes that once sparkled with life now reflected anguish as his friends recalled the warmth of their families, the laughter of children, and the soothing embrace of loved ones long gone or distant. As others plunged into a spiral of regret, recounting their past sins and missteps, Karnik took a different approach. While they surrendered to despair, he shifted his focus towards the flickering flame of possibility. He reviewed every detail of their predicament, his mind racing to calculate potential avenues for escape. In his heart, he harboured a fierce belief that hope could thrive even in the direst of circumstances. Rather than succumb to tears, which would only cloud his vision and weaken his resolve, he stood resolute, his eyes dry, exuding a strength that seemed to embolden those around him.

VIII
THE FACT CHECKER BECOMES GOD'S AMBASSADOR

KARNIK:

While everyone cried and panicked, I was thinking of how to survive. Smoke emerged. It was black and heavy. Disgusting! While reasoning, my sharp eyes caught sight of a window on the wall, facing another block. It was a private one. Not private, but ULTRA PRIVATE! Because I couldn't see through it but knew where it was facing. (due to its location)

It was also locked with a lock, specifically an ancient lock. It was so surprising. I knew we wouldn't be able to open it. So I entered a class, took a chair, and smashed it on the window! With the glass shards, the chair too went flying down 2 floors. Fortunately or unfortunately, no one was down there.

The noise of glass fragmenting caught everyone's attention. They were stunned to see this and were confused. They stopped crying and started to sleuth me. It was around 300 seconds that they interrogated me.

I gazed out of the window. My sight caught a familiar guy on the other block. He was the fact-checker. Indeed, he was Nithin! He was seated near the window. With my whole potential, I shouted his name. But he never turned towards us. Ah! The frustration was taking over me. That block was around 40 metres away. And, he never bothered to see the burning block.

Vivaan shared an idea. He says if we throw something on or near him, he will surely bother to see who did it. His idea was impressive but there was a setback. We should inform him about the situation. Rishan had some plans to deal with it. He quickly brought 10-12 charts and a marker from the nearby classrooms. GENIUS!

Vivaan and I raided nearby classrooms and grabbed whatever we got in our hands. I brought erasers, staplers (emptied) and pouches. But Vivaan had some different plans. He only believed in violence. He brought water bottles and lunch bags! I just admired the consequences if the steel containers or the lunch bag hit his head. Thinking about this gave me goosebumps. I didn't waste any time and started throwing things at Nithin.

Vivaan didn't start violence by now. But later my materials got over and started throwing 'violent' stuff that Vivaan had collected. I forgot about the loss I was giving to the students whose materials we were throwing. Neither of my friends nor Ms Laswell helped me or Vivaan. Rishan was writing some messages on the chart.

Finally, after throwing 40 things, a steel bottle hit his arms. Nithin's expression had a mix of perplexion and wrath. He turned towards the window in fury, probably to scold. He finally saw me. I raised my hand, he too raised his hand. I waved my hand, he too waved his hand. My classmates predicted the cause of my happiness and started to jump in joy.

I think he saw the heavy smoke clouds in the air near our block. Rishan passed me a chart and he told me to show it to him. In the chart, it was written as;

"WE ARE STUCK HERE"

Rishan passed me another chart,

"FIRE BROKE OUT IN MY BLOCK"

Rishan gave me another chart,

"BOTH STAIRCASES ARE UNUSABLE"

Another,

"HELP US!"

I hoped he understood our message. As soon as he read the last one, he moved from his place. Maybe he went to call someone.

He came back, but not alone, he came back with a teacher. The teacher was frightened to see us trapped. She quickly ran outside the class and many students crowded the window (Nithin's classroom). The smoke started to fill in the corridor and we started to cough. We opened the doors and windows of all the accessible classrooms. The smoke started to escape. The fire was spreading rapidly, gradually weakening our school infrastructure. We all soaked our kerchieves and masked them around our faces.

I raised my hand to check the time from my wristwatch. It timed 2:17. By now the fire brigadeers would've arrived. Some sort of whooshing sound filled my ears. I recognised this sound. It was the sound of water jets spraying! Fire Brigade was here! There was complete silence. Only the sound of fire and whooshing was audible.

Our hopes were fulfilled when we saw the fire truck! The fire brigade was here to save us! Along with them, I spotted some ambulances and police patrolling vehicles. We were saved! We got a second life in real terms!

IX

WE GOT A SECOND LIFE

The ladder of the fire truck extended up to the window. A firefighter jumped out from the ladder carriage to the corridor. He shook our hands and explained how to climb down from the ladder. First, the girls went down, then we boys. At last, Ms Laswell climbed down. As soon as she reached the ground, other firefighters climbed up and proceeded to tackle the fire.

Before we could even celebrate our survival, the paramedics surrounded us, transferred us into the ambulance and revved to the CSG Hospital. On the way, we were made to wear oxygen masks to purify the air in our lungs. In the hospital, they took our lung tests and checked for burns. They allowed purified air in our lungs.

Fortunately, there were no traces of any type of problem or disease. But the fate followed Ms Laswell. She sustained Stage-2 Lung Cancer. It was very hard to digest this news. But in the end, "Truth is always bitter."

As soon as I exited the check-up room, I came across my parents. My mother hugged me tightly with tears in her eyes. It was around 210 seconds until she left me. My father was on standby, adoring me. I also saw the parents of my other friends. They too, were in a state of happiness. Along with them, our school principal, headmistress, class teacher and trustee were present in the hospital. They all met personally with every student in my class. But our director sir was missing. How?

DIRECTOR OF GVPS:

Burning block of GVPS

Luckily, all the students and Ms Laswell were rescued successfully by the brigadiers. Even the fire was extinguished by the fire brigade. The brigadiers went inside the block for inspection. All the other students belonging to the burnt block were sent to the auditorium. After an hour or two, the brigadiers stated that the building was unsafe to use. They also mentioned that it would take a minimum of 10-15 days to repair the damage that occurred. They stated that the 2nd floor was completely inaccessible.

There were complex chitters everywhere. There were mixed expressions of students in the auditorium. Some panicked and tensed, while others were playful. This showed the diversity among the students. I was in a confusion about whether being happy seeing the diversity or be sad about the tragedy.

Before I could even think anything about the tragedy, a group; Precisely, a MEGA-GROUP! of raging parents entered our school premises. They were protesting and demonstrating against the school. They were chanting several slogans on the protection of their children. There were around 800 of them!

One among them approached to me in vigour. He was their representative and asked me several questions. He asked about how it happened, why it happened, where it happened when it happened, etc., etc. He had a French beard and had a brown face with decent hair. His questions were more complicated than my thoughts itself. But one question, grabbed my attention, "Was it a deliberate fire?"

Some thoughts prevailed in my mind. It drifted me away to my childhood. Once, when I was in eighth, a similar kind of fire broke out and we were made to sit in the aangan. (Ground) That time, we got to know that it was an intentional fire lightened by an enemy of the school trustee.

Wait. Yes, this fire could be intentional because the sprinkler system didn't work. And we had passed the fire-safety norms the previous week. Brigadiers said that the explosion occurred in the Chemistry lab. And the lab had blast-resistant cylinders and equipment. It was crystal clear that this was a well-planned crime.

Who could it be? why would someone hurt our students and damage the school infra? Will that rascal do the same again? If yes, how? and where? Many such questions prevailed in my ming, making myself more complicated.

X

DIRECTOR GOES TO APDI

The question of the French bearded man made me restless. He had a point in his question. Because just before two weeks we had checked the sprinkler systems. There was no chance of malfunction in it. Moreover, the firefighters stated that the fire started from the Chemistry lab. Which was impossible as we had a world-class lab with fire-resistant types of equipment.

All these thoughts concluded that the fire was a DELIBERATE one. But why? Who could it be? Why only 9-E? Was it a coincidence or conspiracy? Ah! My head was bursting and was paining like dinosaurs were jumping on my head.

Now, there was only one way to find out about it. APDI. Yes, APDI. I will go to APDI (Academy of Prime Detectives of India). They will definitely solve this case and punish that rascal! I stepped out of the taxi and paid him the fare. It was drizzling. The 9-storey dashing building was covered with glass. It was located on a model road and looked more beautiful while it was drizzling. It was inaugurated only a month ago.

As soon as I entered the building, The Jasmine-Lavender fragrance tickled my nose. The furniture was modern and sleek. Mostly white. The Air Conditioners were working and created a pleasant environment. The Coimbatore APDI was the only one in South India, so it was made as large as possible.

NARRATOR:

The Academy of Prime Detectives of India is one of the most vital departments in the world. It handles highly risky cases related to smuggling and counter-insurgency operations. It works hand in hand with other departments. It has some special permissions which other departments don't. APDI has specialised groups called the 'HAWKS'. Hawks have permission to fire on criminals, interrogate them, search places, take them in judicial custody, etc. without the need for permission. Hawks also conduct special operations and counter-insurgency operations.

It is an independent dept. APDI's main headquarters is located in Mumbai, which is an 11-storey building! There are only 6 APDI headquarters in India. They are:

1. Mumbai
2. Coimbatore
3. Noida
4. Dhanbad
5. Nagpur and
6. Guwahati

MUMBAI APDI

The second largest APDI headquarters is located in Coimbatore. It is so because it is the only APDI in South India. All 6 APDIs work coordinatively and can also conduct actions in the range of other APDIs. Like, Mumbai APDI can conduct actions in Bangalore without any problems. (Note: Bangalore comes under the range of Coimbatore APDI).

But why only Coimbatore, not other major cities like Chennai, Bangalore or Hyderabad? There is a special reason for this. Coimbatore lies on the border of Tamil Nadu and

Kerala. We can enter Kerala only by passing the Ghats. Which is very tough to cross and drive. But, there is a flat section in between. It is the Palakkad gap, which is found on the borders of Palghat and Coimbatore. The Palghat gap is a very important pass in India. It is the only flat land that connects the whole of India to Kerala. This pass can only be accessed through Coimbatore only.

The Palakkad gap is a 25-kilometer-wide stretch of flat land, which allows trade and transportation to Kerala easily. The Western Ghats isolates the whole of Kerala from India. It is a very beneficial route, but it is very less supervised. Making it the gateway for illegal immigrants and contraband.

Kerala has been the gateway to smuggled products for ages through its ports. Kerala has become the centre of the black market. The unloaded contraband is to be transported to the whole country. Smugglers choose Coimbatore because of its ease of transportation. Many illegal immigrants enter Coimbatore through the Palghat gap, increasing the crime rates in Coimbatore. This made Coimbatore a communally sensitive city and unsafe. This made the APDI establish its headquarters in Coimbatore for South India.

Coimbatore APDI

Various detectives and their hawks were transferred to Coimbatore from the other APDIs. The Mumbai APDI played a major role in establishing the Coimbatore APDI. The senior detective of Coimbatore APDI is Karan. He was transferred to Coimbatore from Mumbai. This 40-year-old agent is as active and fit as a 25-year-old agent.

APDI Karan has solved more than 500 cases and counting. (Note: Only in 13 years of his career, solved 500+ cases) The previous year, he had headed one of the most dangerous smuggling case in India. (Read the book 'A

PRIME DETECTIVE' to know about the case.) The following is a small gist of the case he headed last year:

It started with the murder of a junior APDI agent. While checking his house, APDI got info about a smuggling racket that killed his whole family. They raided around 4-5 locations in Mumbai and found that the biggest base was located in Coimbatore. The hawks of Karan, Surya and Oberoi raided the biggest profounded smuggling base. As soon as raided, the city of Coimbatore witnessed serial bombings across the city. While they were in Coimbatore, APDI raided the other bases in India. The boss of the whole smuggling racket was APDI Karan's college friend, Manjit.

In this case, more than 25 bases were raided and 1050 smugglers were jailed. More than   ₹10000 crore cash, 3000 guns, 1000 kg of RDX and many more things were seized! Woah! It was further known that the serial bombings and the train derailment were deliberately done by a terrorist outfit, that Manjit funded to do this. More than 600 people died and more than 1500 of them were injured.

Manjit was declared an International Most-Wanted criminal and was arrested by APDI. He was further given a death sentence for treason and murdering hundreds of people. He was the biggest enemy of Bharat.

Manjit was hanged, but there was restlessness in the country, but was controlled. Manjit never thought of people even for once. Those were the darkest days of Coimbatore. Manjit was only one, but there would be many Manjits in the country.

This was the case handled by APDI Karan. The Mumbai APDI decided to transfer Karan, Surya, Oberoi and their hawks to Coimbatore.

THE INVESTIGATION

APDI Karan investigates into the case.

XI

THE SANDALWOOD CHASE

APDI KARAN:

The speedometer showed 110 km/hr. I was on the highway, chasing a sandalwood-laden truck, which was moving at the speed of 110 kmph! We were the lone drivers on the highway. Along with me, Surya too was chasing the truck. The truck was heading towards Tiruppur. We have been chasing the truck for half an hour. I hated these kinds of early mornings.

The highway and truck

Surya was driving parallel to my car. The car was in the middle of the 4-lane side. Aarav was sitting beside me. (Aarav is Karan's hawk) I took my walkie-talkie and discussed the plan with Surya to stop that furious driver. I said,

"Hey man, how the truck is running at 110?"

"Maybe some illegal modifications," Surya replied.

"Okay, I have a plan,"

"What?"

"I will accelerate my car almost to the rear of the truck and Aarav will jump out of the car to the truck."

"Isn't it risky?"

"It is, but no choice."

"Affirmative"

"Over and out."

Aarav was staring at me in confusion. He agrees to our plan. I explained everything to Aarav. The time came. I opened the large sunroof of my car and the rays of light filled my car. Still speeding at 115, Aarav climbed above and balanced, with his confirmation, I throttled the car to the rear of the truck. What will happen if the truck driver applies sudden brakes? The answer was simple- either heaven or hell!

APDI AARAV:

The wind was brushing past me and the smell of sandalwood made me return to the mission. I steadily descended to the bonnet. **CAUTION**☠?- Never keep your hands on the bonnet of a car that has been at the speed of 110 for the past 30 minutes! You can lose your hands due to the heat! Luckily, I balanced on the bonnet without the help of my hands. The truck was only a jump of 2 meters away. Not a big deal. But on a moving car and a truck at 110, a VERY BIG DEAL!

I jumped with my whole stamina and reached the rear of the truck. The sandalwood fragrance was intense and tickled my nose to sneeze. I MADE IT! I made it safely! I slowly walked to the side of the truck. I felt pity for the driver because he could not take sharp turns at 120 and topple me. The driver noticed me and started to throw things at me. I took my pistol and shot the side mirror to frighten the driver.

I slowly came near the door. Now the driver was at gunpoint. He opened the door with full force to topple me but I was not in front of the door. I was near the door. HAHAHAHAHAHAAAA........ I shot the hand of a co-passenger (smuggler) in the truck. Which feared the driver and he slowly stopped the truck.

Still the driver at gunpoint, I asked him for the truck keys. He gave it. I asked them to get out of the truck. They didn't agree. One shot in the air, they agreed and got down. Karan sir and Surya sir came out of their car. Both, the driver and the co-passenger were at gunpoint. Karan and Surya sir checked for the sandalwood. There should be a minimum of 12 tonnes.

"Sandalwood in." Surya sir commented.

"About 13-14 tonnes." Karan sir added.

"So, who will transport the truck to Coimbatore APDI?" I asked them.

"Where is that sleepy-head Raghu?" Karan sir asked.

"Dozing off in my car, maybe" Surya sir added.

Raghu was a truck driver whom the APDI had hired to transport the contraband from one location to the other. Raghu was a sleepy head. He had been unimaginably sleeping for the past two hours in which, we were driving at 110 for 40 minutes straight. Raghu was impossible. Sometimes I doubt his presence in APDI. He also has the capability to sleep during a roller-coaster ride. But, he has the capacity to drive a truck for 60 hours straight! He was very loyal to us.

APDI KARAN:

Aarav walked to Surya's car and brought Raghu. I said to Surya,

"Raghu is impossible, bro,"

"Yeah. How a person can sleep in peace for 40 minutes straight in a car at the speed of 110?"

"I doubt his presence sometimes."

Aarav and Raghu came onto the scene.

"What had happened? Where are we? Why are we here?" Raghu asked us while he rubbed his eyes.

"We were chasing a sandalwood-laden truck for 40 minutes. We are maybe at Tiruppur right now." I answered.

"Okay, I will bring the truck to APDI safely," Raghu assured.

We carried the goons in our cars and reached the Coimbatore APDI in almost an hour. TIRED!

XII

THE SCHOOL VANDAL

I reached Coimbatore by 11 AM and pushed those goons into the lockup. The day grew cloudy and it started to drizzle. I was busy with my work when I heard a knock on the cabin door. I allowed and a short man in his forties entered my cabin. He had short hair and his face was clean shaved. He wore a black pant and a dark purple shirt.

"May I come in sir?" The man asked.

"Yes."

He entered my cabin and introduced himself. His name was Niren and he was the director of GVPS. It was a very renowned school and was in the headlines for the past few days.

"How may I help you sir? I asked Niren.

"Actually, there are a string of incidents which are disturbing our school environment. I feel it is done intentionally."

"So, what happened, sir?"

"About a month ago, one of the steel panels used for roofing, fell, almost killing a student. The main point is that the steel panels were repaired only a week before it fell."

"Oh!"

"And yesterday, one of our Chemistry Labs exploded, burning one-fourth of the block. The fun fact is, 10 days ago, all the fire systems were checked and repaired. Also, the Chem lab was made with modern fire-resistant types of equipment, making it impossible to explode."

My eyes wide-opened. I asked the director for the proof and he showed me all the documents of repair and reports with specific dates written.

"Was the fire fatal?" I asked.

"No, but one of our teachers, Ms Laswell detected lung cancer."

"Oh! It is sadful. Any other crucial information, sir?"

"Yeah, all the time, the victims were the students of class 9-E"

"Strange"

"Sir, please catch those criminals soon, sir. It is the question of the safety of our students and our reputation."

"Any enemies?"

"No, sir,"

"OK, I assure you that I will personally handle this case and catch the psychopath behind it."

"Thank you, sir"

He left my cabin, leaving perplexity in my mind. Why would anyone harm school-going children? Why particularly 9-E? There were many questions in my mind. I was confused about where to start the investigation. My head was exploding an overflowing of questions.

I took a deep breath and moved out of my office. Entered my car and throttled towards GVPS.

The school was bustling, except for the burnt block. I directly went to the principal of the other block to analyse the CCTV. We exchanged greetings and introduced ourselves. I directly came to the point,

"I hope you remember yesterday's tragedy, mam."

"Yes sir, how can I forget that smoky day? It was a smoky tragedy!"

"So, can I view yesterday's CCTV footage of the burnt block?"

"Yes, sure. Just a minute sir, I will search for the folder."

The principal moved the mouse and made some clicks. A cold sweat passed down her cheeks.

"The storage of the whole school network is gone!"

"What!"

"Yes sir, even the educational materials, student information, everything is gone, sir!"

"Check the recycle bin"

"Nothing is there!"

"Oh my god! Meaning the culprit is smart"

"But these materials can only be accessed from school premises."

"Meaning, the criminal is someone from the....."

"School" The Principal completed the sentence for me. There was complete silence in the cabin. There was bafflement filled in the room.

"Okay, it is time for me to leave. Thank you for dedicating your precious time to bring some lead to the case." I thanked her.

"It's my pleasure to help you, sir." She got up and thanked me.

I left the principal's room and boarded my car. I left the school behind. While driving, I received a call from a man. He claimed to be the father of one of the victims of the tragedies in the school. He was Karnik's father.

XIII
THE EVIDENCE OF KARNIK

I drove to Karnik's house. I reached his house and rang the doorbell. His mother opened the door. She allowed me in and offered tea with biscuits. I requested Karnik's parents to leave the room and asked Karnik to stay there. I asked Karnik,

"So, tell me why did you all go to the second floor?"

"Sir, the previous days, the smart board was tampered several times when no one was there in the classroom. On the day of tragedy, the smart board became faulty and Ms Laswell decided to take us to 8-C."

"Hmmmm........ The criminal is a real conspirer. He is too clever than he should be."

"Yeah"

"So, Karnik, do you remember how the fire spread or started?"

"Sir, it was 15-20 minutes to lunch when two unknown peons hit each other, spilling a bucket full of oil. They bo..."

"Wait, why one among them was carrying oil?"

"Sir, besides 8-C is the storeroom. Maybe for some puja. But one thing was suspicious, sir,"

"What?"

"Sir, both the peons were unknown to us. After the collision, they went down and never returned. The fire spread through the oil and the furniture, sir."

"Got it! Those two peons were hired by the psychopath to harm you by spilling the oil in front of the class and exploding the chem lab so that all of you die of burns, suffocation and irritation."

"Yes sir, you are incredible!"

"So, can you tell me about the shed collapse?"

"Yes sir, it happened when we were rehearsing for the assembly on the stage. It was morning time when we were practicing for the assembly on the stage. There was one thing suspicious about the shed fall. The edges of the steel panel were tampered with and cut the steel panel."

"Oh! Was there anyone who got under the panel?"

"Yes, my classmate Karan."

"Oh!"

"Yeah, he luckily managed to hide beneath the desk placed there, after he spotted the panel crashing down. He miraculously survived."

"Woah!" My eyes wide-opened. This detail gave me goosebumps.

"Do you want to share any other points?" I asked Karnik.

"No sir, I don't feel I have any more points to share."

"OK, Karnik, your intriguing detail is very impressive. Thank you Karnik for calling me and leading me in this case."

"Thank you, sir, for paying a visit to me and leading this case. Thank you, sir."

I left his house with no leads. But I had one confusion. How did the criminal reach the shed to tamper it? If he managed to do it, how did he cut the steel without making noise?

To clear this doubt, I revved to 'S.C.K. Steel Works'. After 20 minutes of driving, I reached there. I directly entered the office and met my friend cum manager of SCK Steel Works, Manish. After 10 minutes of gossip, I came to the point.

"Hey, I have a doubt, Manish," I asked.

"What doubt, Karan?"

"Actually, I wanted to know whether we can cut steel shed without making any noise?"

"No, it is impossible!"

"Oh! Then how he could have cut that panel?"

"What panel?"

He was clueless about the case I was handling so I explained to him the case'

"Hmmmm........ Smart!" Manish commented.

"Yeah"

"Maybe the noise of cutting the steel would've fainted by any other noise in the neighbourhood like construction activities."

"Yes! Maybe, I will go right now and check for that! Thanks, Manish! Bye!"

I rushed out and drove to GVPS. I met the director and asked about any construction going on. He said that a neighbourhood was being constructed nearby. I got it. The noise of the construction fainted the noise of cutting the steel panel. I didn't go to the construction site but the noise was clearly audible.

While observing the burnt block, I saw that there was a jungle area and the trees were tall enough. The criminal would've easily climbed the tree and reached the shed. I asked the director,

"Can we visit the forest near the affected block?"

"I think," The director replied.

"Can we go?"

"Yes"

We left for the nearby jungle site. We passed through the main gate and entered the jungle site with the permission of the owner of that piece of land. I scanned the area. Anyone could enter the site. The trees were tall enough to reach the top of the steel shed. I tried to climb the tree. There were grooves and holes that made the climb easy. The grooves and holes were clearly artificial.

There was no chance of getting any clues. I spent some time searching for clues. Weeks of rain would've vanished all the clues. I then visited the construction site. I also observed the construction site. The noise was enough to faint the noise of cutting the steel shed. Luckily, the contractor was present there in the site. I introduced myself and explained about the case. He called the main worker. The main worker too, had no idea about who did it.

The construction site

We also asked all the workers but got no leads. They also didn't have CCTV cameras either. The path seemed to come to a dead end. There was no way I would quit the case. But without any evidence, witness, analogy, anecdote or past experiences, it was impossible to find the psycho. It was the first time I was about to fail any case.

I was leaving the construction site half-heartedly. Suddenly, I spotted a beggar wounded badly. I rushed to him and covered his stomach to stop the blood flow. I analysed that he was stabbed. I carried him on my shoulders. I sprinted to my car with the wounded on my shoulder. I placed him in the back seat and I entered the driving seat.

I revved my car out of the school lane and entered the main road. I broke many red signals and I almost hit a truck. I shifted the gears from 2 to 3, 3 to 4 and then 4 to 5! I was at a staggering speed of 85 kmph! Driving at 85 kmph, on a busy main road at 2 noon! The experience was as exhilarating as it was dangerous.

DISCLAIMER☠?: Never go above 35 or 40 kmph on a busy road.

• 73 •

XIV

FIGHTING FOR LIFE

The beggar was coughing badly and the 'river of life' was gushing out from his incised wounds. I reached the CSG Hospital in just 5 minutes! A stretcher was already arranged as it was informed already. They directly took him to the OT. Hours and hours went by. The OT's doors opened. The doctor rushed to me.

"Sir, the patient is extremely critical. He was badly stabbed 3 times. The wounds are very deep. We need blood, sir." The doctor said.

"Don't you have it in the blood bank?" I questioned.

"No, sir, we don't. It is the rarest blood group in the world. He is RH-Null and only 50 people on this planet possess this blood group."

"Ahhhhh!!!!!!!! How many hours can he live?!!!!!"

"Hardly 30 minutes." The doctor replied, ashamed.

"Okay, okay..... Can he talk to me? Any chance?"

"Sorry sir, he is unconscious and there is no way he can live." Tears dropped from the eyes of the doctor while he talked to me. I was speechless and tears rushed from my eyes. I cried for 5 minutes and requested the doctor to send the dead body to APDI for post-mortem. The beggar was the only option, through which I could further investigate the case. I left the hospital with regret. Being an APDI agent, I wasn't able to save a citizen of my country. I drank my anger and rode to the APDI. My car was stinking of blood. So, I gave my car to the car washing dept. Of APDI. Yeah, APDI has a separate car-washing unit.

I entered my cabin and sat on the chair. I tried to relax myself by deep-breating but, whenever my eyes closed, the face of that poor beggar flashed. It was hard to forget that incident. I rang my phone to CSG Hospital and reminded them about the transfer of the body of that beggar. I hung up the phone. I went down to check for my car. Full clean. I entered my car and drove to the construction site where the beggar's was found.

Blood stains, cloth pieces, bad smell and flies. How none of the workers noticed him. Maybe the beggar was stabbed somewhere else and was shifted here. There were many possibilities. I collected all the evidences I was able to get.

Some thoughts prevailed in my mind, which made me go to the school. There, I met the security guard once again. He guarded the gate through which cabs and rickshaws entered. I asked him whether any unknown person entered the ground along with the drivers. He thought for some time and said, "Yes sir, once I saw a man along with a rickshaw driver just before the day of fire. I don't remember the person's or the driver's face. Also, I don't remember if he left the school premises."

It would've been difficult to find that man if I hadn't spotted a camera in a house, opposite the gate. Luckily, there wasn't a lock in the house. I rang the doorbell. A girl of 6-7 years opened the door and called for her father.

We introduced ourselves and requested him to allow me to review the CCTV footage of Feb 2. He guided me with the computer and opened the folder of the footage. I took my pen drive, connected it to the computer and transferred the footage to the pen drive. I thanked him and left his house.

After reaching the APDI, I opened my laptop and inserted the pen drive. I opened the footage of Feb 2 and reviewed it. At around 3:37, I spotted 2-3 rickshaws. A man was sitting with the rickshaw driver in vehicle number 'TN 99 FI 2445'. I noted the number in my diary and paused the footage. I reversed the footage and paused when the man's face was clear. I clicked the photo of that man. The man's face was clear and I sent it to the ID team of APDI for identification.

After a few minutes, I received a call from the ID team. They confirmed that the man was Rehan. He had past criminal records like chain snatching. His address was confirmed that he lived in Podanur. According to the ID team, Rehan had no family and worked as a daily wage labourer.

I then confirmed the footage and noticed that he never exited the school. I took my car keys and drove to Rehan's house. I reached his house by 6. He lived on the 3rd floor of a poorly maintained apartment. It had no CCTV cameras. I knocked on his door 5-6 times but I received no answer. Only one option left. I moved 5 steps backwards, and with my whole might I ran towards the door and kicked the door. The door opened. The paint in the house was not in good condition. The ceiling wasn't good and the PoP (Plaster of Paris) was coming out. In the name of furniture, there was only a bed and a steel cupboard. There was a separate kitchen, but not that good.

Rehan's apartment

XV
A NOT SO SMALL SURPRISE

With my gloves on, I started to look for clues. Kitchen-nothing special; Hall-nothing special. The real game started when I opened the cupboard. As I opened it, a strong fragrance of Jasmine tickled my nose, which was suspicious. As I ran through the clothes, I found a bag full of cash and a high-end laptop. How could a daily wage labourer own a laptop?

At the topmost shelf of the cupboard, there was a brown sac where 4-5 flies were roaming. As soon as I brought the sac down, chills spread out in my spine when I discovered a dead body in it! It was truly confusing and frightening! It was cruelly horrific. The body was chopped into pieces! NASTY! It was the worst murder I have ever seen in my life.

Rehan's room

I quickly called the APDI. They reached in 20 minutes. For sure, Rehan was hired by someone else to ignite the fire and collapse the shed. Who would've hired him? How will we find him?

I went near the cupboard and tried to move it, but I wasn't able to move it. I quickly called one of the investigators and with his help, we moved the cupboard. There was an ungrilled window behind the cupboard. Now I was able to visualise the murder. The murderer climbed 3 floors, entered Rehan's room through the window, and killed Rehan in pieces, put them in a sac, placed it in the cupboard and poured air freshener. But why did the murderer put the sac in the cupboard? Maybe it was too heavy to carry 3 floors down and someone would've noticed if thrown.

He then tied the cupboard with a rope in such a way that it would untie when wanted. He pulled the cupboard from outside the window when placed perfectly, he would've untied it and closed the window. The murderer was a professional for sure. But not that good because he left his traces on the platform outside the window. There were shoeprints on it. In bonus, there was a cloth piece at the window with blood on it.

I quickly took photos and asked Aarav to take the sample of blood and the cloth piece. Finally, some lead in the case. They took the samples for testing in the laboratory. I went down and stood exactly below the window of Rehan's room.

There, I searched for other evidences. To my surprise, there were footprints, the exact size I found on the window platform. I followed it. The footprints faded and tyre marks emerged. I quickly took a photo and measured it. I followed the tyre marks. The main road emerged and the tyre marks were discontinued. But the tyre marks only discontinued after taking a left from the apartment.

After spending some time investigating, I left for APDI and reviewed the CCTV footage of Traffic Police near the apartment. Around 4 PM, I spotted a bike exiting the apartment to the left. I paused the footage and matched the tyre design with the one in the CCTV. Matched. I noted the bike's number 'AB 37 NA 2812'. I shifted to the next camera, it took a right at the junction. Next camera, it went straight. It took a right at the next unction. It went straight and finally stopped there and entered a house. I fast-forwarded it and set it to live footage. He never exited.

I ordered the official to check the footage and update me if any changes occurred. I updated the location of that house in the GPS. I boarded one of the bikes of APDI and throttled to the location.

XVI
WINDS OF VENGEANCE ON ASPHALT

After a smooth drive on the motorcycle, I reached the location by 8:30. It was pitch dark and extremely silent. Maybe the silence was the silence before the disaster. Cold sweat passed through my cheeks. I spotted the bike and the house. I took my pistol in my hand and slowly tried to open the door. The door opened. I stepped inside and turned on the flashlight built into the pistol.

I heard some noise behind me. As I turned, my pulse quickened. A figure sprinted towards the bike, his intentions unmistakable. Instinct kicked in—I bolted after him, the adrenaline surging through my veins like wildfire. But before I could close the gap, the roar of the engine cut through the air. He was already on the bike, throttling it to life.

Without hesitation, I lunged for the APDI's bike, barely swinging my leg over before igniting the engine. The machine roared beneath me as I twisted the throttle, the tyres screeching against the pavement as I took off in pursuit. The murderer had a head start, but I wasn't about to let him escape.

The engine screamed as I accelerated, the world around me blurring. At an unbelievable 100 kmph, the wind slammed into me like a wall, biting through my jacket and sending chills racing down my spine. My fingers tightened on the handlebars as I shifted gears, the bike surging forward. The killer ahead was skilled—too skilled. His sharp turns and fluid movements screamed experience. He was no amateur.

The chase tore through the outskirts, where the open road allowed us to push the limits. But then came the twist: the main road loomed ahead, a chaos of congested traffic. I cursed under my breath. The labyrinth of cars and buses could be either a blessing or a death trap.

The bike chase

But the murderer showed no signs of hesitation. Weaving through the vehicles with alarming precision, he maintained a blistering 60 kmph, the gap between us fluctuating dangerously. My instincts screamed for caution, but there was no room for doubt. Matching his speed, I manoeuvred through the congested road, the exhaust's growl reverberating between the walls of vehicles. The tension was palpable; one wrong move, and it would all be over.

Suddenly, the stakes soared. The traffic slowed, then halted entirely, transforming the road into a frozen battlefield. My mind raced. The murderer used the standstill to his advantage, veering sharply into a narrow alleyway without losing momentum. The decision was instant—I followed him, the bike's tyres skidding slightly as I leaned into the turn.

The alley was claustrophobic, the walls on either side flashing past in a blur. The thunderous echoes of our exhausts ricocheted off the concrete, startling pedestrians who scrambled to safety. My heart pounded as the risk amplified; one slip, and I'd be thrown into the unforgiving walls.

Emerging from the lane, he veered onto a model road, his audacity reaching new heights as he mounted the footpath. I gritted my teeth. This wasn't just a chase—it was a game of brinkmanship, with both of us daring to push the limits of our mortality. I mirrored his move, the bike jolting as it hit the uneven surface.

Pedestrians screamed and scattered, the chaos amplifying the stakes. Every second felt stretched, every turn a gamble. I couldn't afford to lose sight of him, but the margin for error was razor-thin. The model road was familiar to me. It was the model road on which APDI was established. The biker was unaware of it. He finally came to a stall when he saw 6 APDI cars blocking his way.

He tried to make a turn but one of the officers shot his leg and the biker fell. I also turned off the engine and got off the motorcycle. I removed my helmet. The spine-chilling chase came to an end. It was a complete thriller chase. Adrenalin stopped flushing.

I handcuffed that dumb biker. I pulled him to the APDI office. His name was Junaid. Junaid accepted that he was the one who murdered Rehan. But he was not ready to give the reason for killing. After torturing for 3 hours, he always said the same thing. "I don't know! I just got 2 lakh cash for killing Rehan!"

Then came the rickshaw driver who dropped Rehan to school. He was Babu. Our team successfully caught him before he left the city. Babu said that an unknown person gave him 50000 rupees to drop Rehan to school. Babu was in need of money and he accepted the proposal. The crime organiser tried his best to conceal his identity.

XVII
SMALL BUT SIGNIFICANT

Junaid and Babu were jailed. I went to Junaid's house for an investigation. Junaid's house was similar to Rehan's. A small rented room with improper furniture. There was a bed, a small kitchen and a cupboard. I opened the cupboard. I opened the cupboard to find tonnes of clothes and other essentials.

There was nothing special in the kitchen. I went to check for the bed. I lifted the mattress and opened the door of the shelf hidden beneath it. I found over four stacks of ₹500 notes. 1 stack contains 100 notes. Meaning, there was 2 lakh cash. Probably, this was the payment for killing Rehan. I took those stacks and dropped them in the evidence pouch. The stacks were covered in the newspapers.

The newspapers dated 2nd November. While dropping the last one, I noticed that a newspaper bill was stuck onto the newspaper. Generally, the newspaper bills are stuck to the front page with gum. In a hurry, the payer forgot to remove the bill. It was a small but significant clue. The newspaper was of 'THE SECULAR' news network. The paper dealer was Samar Mistri, whose office was located in RS Puram. These details were on the bill. When I flipped the bill, 'SC Anna' was written on it. Meaning, he was the one who read this newspaper.

I drove to the 'MISTRI PAPERS', Samar's office. He was available there. I knocked on his door and entered. He welcomed me and introduced himself. I showed him the newspaper's front page, to which the bill was stuck. He thought for a few seconds and recalled SC Anna. With a shine on his face, he exclaimed,

"SC Anna meant Sarohan Chinnampalli! He is a regular reader of 'THE SECULAR'"

"Can I get his address?"

"Yeah, sure."

He searched for his name in his laptop. He wrote his address on a paper and gave it to me.

"Thank you, Samar, you have helped me a lot," I thanked him.

"It's my pleasure. Please do visit again, sir."

"Bye"

I left his office and called Surya. I let him know about the case I handled and asked him to arrive at *Chinnampalli Residence.* I also asked him to bring his hawks together. I left for SC's residence. Surya and his hawks were ready at the boundary of SC's residence.

Chinnampalli Residence

I wore my hawk gear. Bullet-proof vest, helmet, night-vision goggles, thick clothing and took the MP-5 Rifle. I slowly opened the gate. 2 of the other hawks took care of the guards at the gate. We parted ways and covered the house from all sides. I rang the doorbell and hid. As soon as the door opened, I jumped and captured the man who opened the door and covered his mouth. He was SC's servant.

I asked for Sarohan and he said that he was sleeping in the drawing room. I threatened him to open all the doors and windows on the ground floor. As soon as he opened them, hawks entered the house and started the *OPERATION BIZMAN*. According to our intel, Sarohan was a businessman, who was accused of operating mafias of Western Tamil Nadu or Kongunadu. This only existed as an allegation.

The hawks silently toppled the security personnel hired by Sarohan. We silently reached to the drawing room and found Sarohan snoring. I caught his hand and pulled him down the sofa. He fell hard on the ground. He quickly stood up and was at gunpoint by four hawks. He didn't wait to be tortured and blurted out the name of the real crime organiser.

He said that he was paid for deliberating the fire and the shed collapse. The name left everyone surprised and jaw-dropped. It was indeed an alias. It was unbelievable and unthinkable! No one was ready to believe it but the 'bitter' truth was discovered. The name gave us chills and goosebumps. The alias was *Narco Phantom X*. No one knew his real name.

Cold sweats passed through my cheeks. No one has ever seen him. If 'anyone' did, that 'anyone' would never exist. He is a drug lord, who the whole of India is searching for. He has maintained his secrecy very well. Though he operates only in Kongunadu, he fears the whole of India. I quickly called APDI for more hawks and forces because the X-Gang might be here any second. After all, we have attacked a person who he knows. He won't leave us!

Surya came from upstairs. He went there to check for any other security personnel. He asked for the crime organiser. When he heard 'Narco Phantom X', a scare was seen in his eyes. Now it was APDI vs. X. It was time for a new operation; *'OPERATION X'!* The main motive of this operation was to eradicate Narco Phantom X's influence in the region. It may sound unreal, but it was the truth.

XVIII

THE OPERATION X

Suddenly, rounds of firings erupted and glass shattered. All took a safe cover within seconds. This warned us of the presence of the X gang. After several rounds of firings, there was complete silence. Now a search operation was converted into a WAR! And the war has to be won by APDI. The reputation of India and APDI was at risk. I heard faint sounds of footsteps to my right. I was ready to fire but before I could even fire, they threw a grenade, which landed at the centre and exploded. Blinding and deafening us for seconds.

Phew! Everyone was safe. I knew we wouldn't be able to fight from the ground floor until additional Hawks arrived. We were left with nothing, but only with few guns.

APDI SURYA:

The whole drawing room was filled with smoke. We had night vision goggles, through which we could partially through smoke. I should make use of the smoke. Yes, I had a risky plan. I talked to Karan through the walkie-talkie. We decided that we would go upstairs and fight from there. We slowly moved towards the stairs in the prone position.

As soon as we came near the stairs, with our whole stamina, we ran upwards; Despite the bullet firings, we managed to reach the first floor safely. I peeped through the window to see around 30-40 X-men waiting outside with arms and ammunition.

To our luck, Karan found a sniper rifle with plenty of ammo. It was not surprising to find this with a man with mafia relations. I took charge of the sniper and Karan handled the MP-5 Rifle. I went to the nearby room and fought from there. Karan hit the X-men on their legs and arms while I killed the one handling grenades. I did my job. I scoped it towards them, before they threw the grenade, I hit the trigger of the sniper and the bullet hit their head. HEADSHOT!

Someone who I didn't notice, threw a grenade at me. I left the sniper and ran to the other room. The grenade blasted. The impact made me fall. The X-men assumed that I was dead and started to celebrate and fired several rounds.

Karan threw smoke grenades on the X-men and started to fire. With his same old precision, he hit their palms and legs. The smoke ran away. The gang members were all down. Fight at a peaceful rich colony was unimaginable and unreal! We both breathed a sigh of relief.

Within a few minutes, the APDI trucks arrived with Hawks. In total, there were three trucks. Three because it carried Hawks and was needed to deport the X-men to APDI. For sure, there will be more people in the X gang.

Because a state-level mafia won't be as small as 30 or 40 members.

APDI KARAN:

Through the window, I spotted 4to 5 large jeeps heading towards us! They were fully packed with X-men with guns! I quickly ran for the sniper and aimed for the 2nd jeep's tyre. They were ready to attack us and the APDI trucks. I hit the trigger and the bullet hit the front-left tyre of the 2nd jeep. The jeep flew in the air and was rotating. It fell on the 1st jeep and all the other jeeps crashed. Surya didn't wait for others and started to fire on those jeeps.

Though crashed, X-men came out with guns. But before they could even fire, the additional Hawks fired at them. There were 60 to 70 X-men. Now we didn't care about hitting palms or legs. We just fired at them. A full-blown war was going on. I assumed that many X-men may come from the backside. So, I went to the other side of the house, still on the 1st floor. My jaw dropped when I saw 7 fully packed jeeps approaching SC's residence. I called Surya to fight them.

But it was the limit when I saw a man with a rocket launcher, which was loaded! Without wasting any time, I aimed for that man, pulled the trigger and the bullet hit the man. Though the bullet hit the man, it didn't stop the rocket from launching. The rocket was LAUNCHED! Fortunately, the rocket hit a jeep of X-men. The jeep flew high in the sky and landed on another jeep. The Hawks down started to fire on the X-men coming out of the jeep.

Surya took his gun and open fired on them (X-men). He reloaded, fired; Reloaded, fired. He did this for around 3 times. The whole room was filled with smoke and the ground with bullet shells. A very wild fight. We fought with around 120 of them! The height gave us an advantage.

By now, the whole country would've known about this war. To be more specific, this type of combat is known as a 'Counter-Insurgency Operation'. Maybe NPX would've also sent forces to the APDI to attack. I called the APDI dept. I got to know that X gang was attacking them. I quickly made a call to CAPDI (Chief of APDI) to order other APDIs to send troops all over Tamil Nadu to stabilise the situation. He agreed to my proposal and also ensured that he would ask the Government of India to send CRPF (Central Reserved Police Force) and RAF (Rapid Action Force) forces to Coimbatore.

Surya and I went down. Everyone was fine. Now the time came to deport SC to APDI. It will be a tough job because X-men are active now. Also, the headquarters was busy fighting. It may seem impossible but APDI is known to do the impossible!

We dragged Sarohan to the APDI truck and the other Hawks too entered the truck. We left some Hawks in SC's residence. I boarded my car with two other Hawks. We all were in a 'ready-to-fight' mode. One truck drove ahead of me, two trucks drove behind me. The truck just behind me contained Sarohan Chinnampalli.

When we were 500 metres to APDI, we stopped. All the Hawks got down, except for four Hawks protecting SC. The truck ahead of me and the truck at the last drove forward and parked diagonally.

I made a call to APDI to know about the situation and asked for their count. They responded they were facing insurgency from 24 X-men. I searched for altitude, from where I could spot all the 24 and kill them. I spotted a 2-storey building with an open terrace. Nice. Escaping the bullets, I entered the house and went straight to the terrace.

There was a clear view. I spotted an X-man with a grenade in his hand, ready to throw. There were 4 X-men near him. I scoped and hit the grenade with the bullet. The grenade exploded, killing 5 X-men. 19 left. The blast distracted the other X-men. Taking this opportunity, Hawks fired on them. 7 more dead. 12 left.

I scoped at the other two X-men near the truck and killed them. I ordered the Hawks hiding behind the truck to advance. As they advanced, they killed 3 other X-men. 7 left. I reloaded my sniper and killed 3 more. Only 4 left. I again ordered the Hawks to advance. 3 more killed. Only 1 X-man was left. I spotted him but he took cover.

Surya did that job for me. He killed that single man. I scanned the area for safety and confirmed that all X-men were down. We celebrated this moment. We all were happy and deported Sarohan to APDI. A fear lasted in my mind. NPX was still free and could organise riots. Being the biggest mafia in Tamil Nadu, he can organise riots and more insurgent actions.

While I was thinking about this, the noise produced by the helicopter emerged. I turned up and saw that CRPF and RAF forces had arrived. The helicopters landed and they came out. They informed us that their other forces had reached the various parts of Tamil Nadu.

CRPF and RAF Helicopers

They took our vehicles and reached different parts of the city to stabilise the situation. As soon as they left, I received a call from APDI. The news which they gave us was very crucial. The hint they gave will be the most useful hint to completely eradicate the X GANG......

XIX

'X', Y, Z..... ENDS

The APDI cracked the location of NPX. But the real name of NPX left us astounded and perplexed. The real name of NPX was Kashan Mirza. You will be shocked to know that he was the trustee of GVPS! SHOCKING! How can this happen? Why will he do it? Why will he harm his own school? It was truly confusing.

APDI found out his location to be in Saibaba Colony, which is one of the most posh areas in the city. The name of his house is *MIRZALAND*. Interestingly, his residence is located near *CHINNAMPALLI RESIDENCE.*

Mirzaland

It was decided that Surya, Oberoi, me and our Hawks would go to *MIRZALAND* and arrest Kashan Mirza. We boarded our vehicles and reached *MIRZALAND*. We stopped our vehicles one kilometre to Mirzaland. We made a plan to enter his house. We made 4 of our Hawks to handle the sniper. Those 4 Hawks were in a radius of 1 kilometre from his residence in all 4 directions. (NOTE: The code names for the snipers: Sniper in North- N1; Sniper in South- S1; Sniper in West- W1; Sniper in East- E1) The snipers hid so well that we too were unable to spot them.

We left 10 of our Hawks in the surroundings of Mirza's residence for others' safety. Now, we 44 Hawks covered the front gate and the back gate. (22 in front, 22 in back) We were ready to fight with the X-men. This could be the last fight of our career. But we were ready to fight.

I was at the front gate while Surya was at the back gate. All the four snipers were ready. The front gate was facing the east direction while the back gate faced the west direction. I ordered E1 to kill the X-men at the main gate. Three of them down. It was nighttime so no one noticed them. I asked E1 for confirmation to enter *MIRZALAND*. He answered in affirmative. In the combat position, I and the 21 other Hawks entered.

We slowly entered and hid in the tall grass and bush. With the confirmation of other Hawks, we started *OPERATION KMX*. Slowly-slowly I advanced and rested on the wall with my back near the main door. Aarav too followed me and rested in the position in which I rested.

I ordered E1 to check for the nearby militants. He confirmed that there were no X-men. I ordered him to shoot the person whoever opened the door. All the other Hawks were in the prone position, hiding between the grass.

I knocked on the door and hid near the door. As soon as the door opened, within 2 seconds, he was down. E1 did a great job! But, as soon as he was dead, the X-men inside the house opened fire on us. Probably AK-47. I asked E1, N1 and S1 to kill the X-men open firing on us. All the 3 snipers answered with a negative, stating that there was no visibility of X-men in the living room.

It was all upon the ground operators (We, Hawks fighting from the ground). I threw two smoke grenades inside and activated the night vision mode. But still, they were open firing. From the side, I spotted an X-man and killed him. Now the firing stopped.

APDI SURYA:

I heard sounds of open firing from the other side. I asked W1 to kill the X-men whoever was dangerous for us. W1 fires 4 shots. Meaning he killed 4 X-men. I asked for his confirmation to enter the house. He affirmated. I opened the door and moved forward slowly with alertness. I swiftly turned to my right and pulled the trigger, killing two X-men, who were ready to fire. I heard footsteps, so I took cover beneath the dining table. The footsteps emerged to my left. When the legs of X-men were visible, I hit the trigger and hit their legs. As soon as they fell. I hit their chests. Two more were encountered.

Now, I heard footsteps to my right. This time, one of the Hawk killed him with the knife. I spotted another X-man in the other room, then another, then another,...... More than 7 X-men were there in that room. I asked S1 to analyse the room for any civilians. S1 confirmed that there were no civilians in the room. I took a grenade, removed the clip and threw it in the room. It blasted with a loud noise, killing all those 7 X-men.

APDI KARAN:

I heard some bullets firing in some gaps and a grenade blasting. Maybe Surya started the operation. While my hawks were firing some shots. I moved to one of the windows and entered the house. Following me, Aarav too entered. We spotted two X-men and killed them. But suddenly, someone hit a wooden chair on my back and someone almost stabbed me. But I escaped, leaving a scar on the right side of my hip. My gun slipped down. I caught his hand and snatched the knife and stabbed him 7 times in his chest.

I picked up my gun and saw my wounded hip. Blood oozed out from my wound but I didn't care about it. Aarav was perplexed about what happened. The whole incident happened only in 5 seconds! We moved forward and found the door to the living room. I inserted a small keyhole camera and saw whatever happened in the living room. I found that there were no civilians and 17 X-men were there.

I ordered one of the Hawk outside to throw 2 smoke grenades and 4 grenades, scattered. He did as follows. Aarav and I went to the farthest end of the room. I also informed Surya about the grenades, so I advised him to be away from the living room. The Hawk did as follows. He threw 2 smoke grenades and after 15 seconds, 4 explosions were heard. The Hawks and I entered the living room and confirmed that all 17 X-men were dead. Surya and I met. The whole of the ground floor. Now only the 1st floor was left.

From the stairs, I threw a smoke grenade to the 1st floor and went there. There was pitch silence. I spotted a leg behind a wall. I slowly moved towards there. When I was close to that wall, I swiftly moved forward. turned to my right. It was KASHAN MIRZA! I quickly shot his leg and his arm and he wailed in pain. With the walkie-talkie, I informed the whole APDI team and the headquarters about the discovery of Kashan Mirza. Now we were to deport Kashan Mirza to APDI safely.

We took him and placed him in the APDI truck. Fortunately, we were able to deport Kashan Mirza to APDI from his residence in Saibaba Colony. The Coimbatore APDI received a call from CAPDI. He informed that the X Gang was eradicated by the CRPF, RAF and APDI forces all across Tamil Nadu. After counting X-men killed here, the total count of X-men was 787! Huge number!

We all jumped in excitement and celebrated this historic counter-terrorism or insurgency operation. The OPERATIONS BIZMAN, X and KMX successfully concluded! We all breathed a sigh of relief.

XX

A SHOCKIN' REVELATION

Mirza was arrested and tortured for days. After days of torture, he revealed the reason for harming his own school. Here's the conversation between Mirza and me,

"So, do you agree that you are the Narco Phantom X and controlled the X gang?" I asked Mirza.

"Yes," He replied.

"What was the need for harming your school, Golden Valley Public School?"

"All I did it for an insurance scam."

"What?"

"Yes,"

"But why?"

"I needed money for a payment of 700 Crore Indian Rupees."

"What payment?"

"The payment to a drug dealer in Colombia."

"Okay. Break down the insurance scam, meaning how did you initiate it and how much you got?"

"From the shed collapse, I received 40 crores and from the fire, I got 600 crores. I had 100 crores extra from my savings as black money."

"Oh! Who all was involved in this?"

"I initiated the shed collapse and the explosion with the help of Rehan and Babu. Rehan cut the shed, placed a small bomb in the cylinder of the Chemistry lab and BOOM!"

"Why did you kill Rehan? But not Babu?"

"Rehan knew my identity but Babu didn't."

"Hmmm...... Why did you target 9-E?"

"To make it look like targeted terrorism, which helped me out further in the insurance scam. With this targeted terrorism, I gained 60 crores."

"Interesting, how did you manage to build back the infra?"

"I bought materials and labour from my shell companies. I inflated the bill more than the actual cost. I managed to build everything back in 50 crores."

"What about legal fees and compensation?"

"I also faked those too,"

"How big is your gang?"

"Around 780 or 790 X-men."

"We found links between you and Inter-Service Intelligence, the ISI, intel agency of Pakistan. Is it true?"

After hours of torture,

"Yes! I admit that I am paid by the ISI to de-stabilise India! I had plans to organise riots in the following year!"

"Okay. Do you have any family?"

"NO."

"Okay"

After months of investigation, it was revealed that Kashan Mirza was paid by ISI and was planning to conduct paid riots in India. He further revealed his business partners in drugs and his bases. All were seized and captured by APDI. The following is the split up of the insurance scam:

TOTAL INSURANCE SCAMMED: 600 CRORES

1. **GENERAL LIABILITY INSURANCE**: 50 CRORES: The harm caused by the school to students and legal lawsuit
2. **PROPERTY INSURANCE**: 300 CRORES: Replace infrastructure on campus.
3. **CYBER LIABILITY INSURANCE**: 40 CRORES: Data breach or deletion of data.
4. **STUDENT INSURANCE**: 25*20=500 LAKHS OR 5 CRORES: Compensation for accidental injuries of students. (Faked the entries)
5. **WORKERS' COMPENSATION INSURANCE**: 15 CRORES
6. **DIRECTORS AND OFFICERS PROTECTION INSURANCE**: 41 CRORES: Protects top officials from their wrong decisions.
7. **BUSINESS INTERRUPTION INSURANCE**: 79 CRORES
8. **TERRORISM INSURANCE**: 70 CRORES: If the campus is targeted.

ABOUT THE AUTHOR

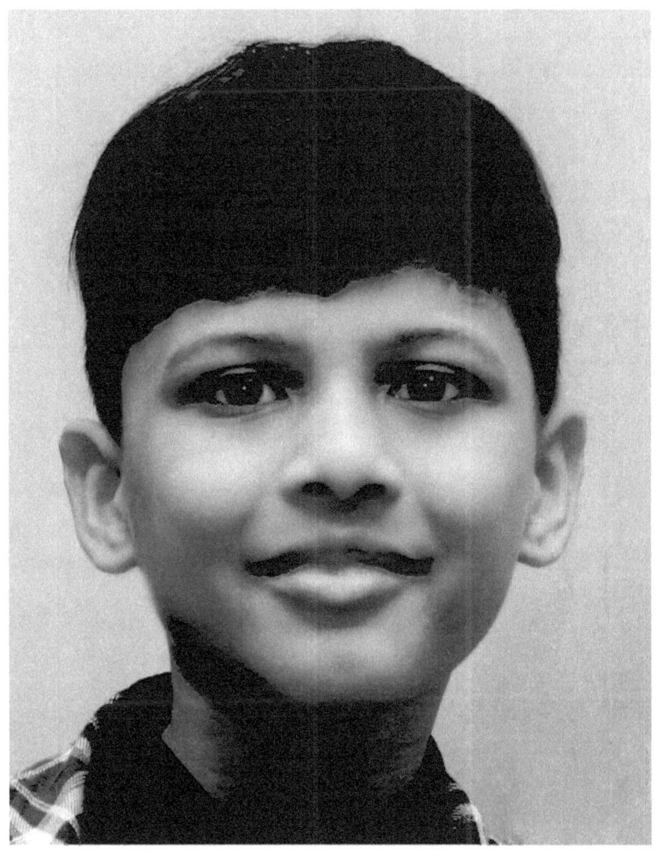

Naman A

Naman was born on December 28th, 2010 to parents Abishek and Keerthi in Coimbatore, India. He currently attends Suguna International School. At just 14 years old, Naman has already written two books, "A Prime Detective" and "A Road Trip to Mumbai," and plans to write many more.

Naman enjoys a variety of sports such as volleyball, football, cricket, basketball, and kho-kho. In his free time, he likes to study, read books, watch television, and play. His favourite hobbies are reading and playing dominoes (not the pizza company, but the toppling game).

Dominoes game

೮〇

Words by the author:

"I hope you liked this story and I expect you to read my further coming books in future. I would suggest you to read my first book, 'A PRIME DETECTIVE' and my second book 'A ROAD TRIP TO MUMBAI'. Thank You."

Your's,

Author: Naman A